Magic Mirror
The Visionary Voyage

Luther Tsai
Nury Vittachi

REYCRAFT

Reycraft Books
145 Huguenot Street
New Rochelle, NY 10801

Reycraftbooks.com

Reycraft Books is a trade imprint and trademark of Newmark Learning, LLC.

Educators and Librarians: Our books may be purchased in bulk for promotional,
educational,or business use. Please contact sales@reycraftbooks.com.

Library of Congress Cataloging-in-Publication Data is available.

Hardcover ISBN: 978-1-4788-6903-0
Paperback ISBN: 978-1-4788-6810-1

Printed in Dongguan, China. 8557/0823/20475

10 9 8 7 6 5 4 3 2 1

First Edition Paperback published by Reycraft Books 2019

Reycraft Books and Newmark Learning, LLC, support diversity and
the First Amendment, and celebrate the right to read.

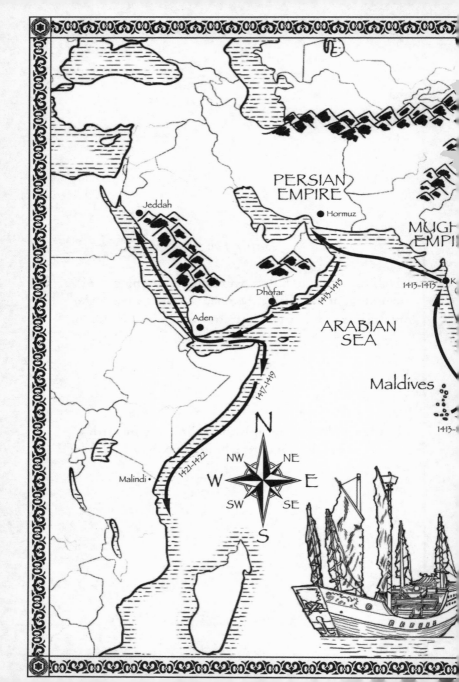

What Is Real?

In this story, facts and whispers of real-life people are here for you to find.

The rest of the story is made up of shadows and reflections, fleeting images of people and events that remain, and haunt us still.

Look inside the Magic Mirror ...

*Now we see but a poor
reflection as in a mirror ...
Now I know in part ...
Then I shall know fully, even
as I am fully known.*

CONTENTS

Page

The Lost Grandfather

Chocolate cake and ice cream for breakfast? Surely not!

Miranda Lee stared crossly at her brother Marko as he stepped out of the kitchen with a bowl piled high with his two favorite desserts.

"What are you doing?"

He sat down at the table and started stirring the contents of his bowl into a gooey, gray mess. "Having breakfast," he said.

"You can't have chocolate cake and ice cream for breakfast," she said, folding her arms.

"Says who?" Marko replied, mumbling through a mouthful of deliciously cold, sweet sludge. "Mama's gone, Dad's not here, and Ye Ye's disappeared."

"Still," said Miranda. She was annoyed, but she was also hungry—and the sweet smell was making her mouth water. Her brother's odd way of thinking usually annoyed her, but she realized that sometimes he stumbled on a good idea—like this one.

Without a word, she raced into the kitchen and helped herself to her own breakfast—chocolate cake and ice cream, with multicolored sprinkles on top.

The two children sat in silence at the living room table, slurping at the illicit breakfast that occupied their attention for almost six minutes.

Using her tongue to remove her ice cream mustache, Miranda sat back with a smile of satisfaction, realizing that delicious things were double-delicious when you had them on unexpected or "wrong" occasions.

But as she tossed the spoon into the empty bowl, the worry that had been at the back of her mind since the previous evening returned to center stage. Where was their grandfather? Ye Ye often disappeared on his travels, sometimes for days on end. But he never went away when he was supposed to be on parent duty at home. That was the rule. He vanished when one or both of their parents were at home. But when their mother and father had business trips, grandfather was at home and in charge of looking after Miranda and her brother.

So where was he? The previous morning, she and her brother had woken to find the house empty.

It was a school holiday, so they simply helped themselves to snacks and spent the day watching television and reading books.

Marko, who was nervous by nature, had started to get worried about the prolonged absence of Ye Ye by midafternoon. His sister had tried to reassure him that nothing was wrong. "He's probably just gone shopping, or he's talking to those old friends of his about the old days—you know what he's like."

But evening had eventually come, and the crumbly, white-walled house on Praya Road remained free of adults.

"When's Ye Ye coming home?" Marko had asked.

"How am I supposed to know?" Miranda had snapped back at him, her own unhappiness making her irritable. But she was the older one (twelve and three-quarters, while he had just turned ten), so it was her job to be responsible and mature.

"Don't worry. I'll make noodles for dinner," she had then added.

His face had brightened.

At nine o'clock that night, she had coaxed him to go to bed, and then she had gone to the front door and scanned the street, up and down. It was dark and deserted. She felt angry. Where was their grandfather? How were they supposed to look after themselves? To make matters worse, their housekeeper, Gwendy, was on her annual vacation, so their grandfather's timing was really off. This was ridiculous! How she would scold him when he got home. She had a good mind to tell Mama and Daddy about it, too, when they returned.

But when would that be? She had no idea.

She stepped out into the garden. The hilltop street on which they lived contained many rather stately houses—but their building looked merely old.

Yes, there was a once-charming timber bridge across a small pool in the garden, but the wood was rotten and the water lilies beneath were shriveled. The hedges had grown out of shape, and many of the trees had lost their leaves. Paint was peeling off the walls of the house. Everything seemed forgotten and unloved.

Miranda had stood on the rotting bridge and felt angry, not for the first time, about how difficult it was to be part of this family. Nothing seemed normal about the Lees. Dad was from America, and Mama from China, and the two children were adopted, so their family should have been a wonderful example of multicultural harmony.

There were several children in her class at school whose super-mixed backgrounds meant that they had more vacations than most kids, and a fantastic range of uncles and aunts who sent gifts from around the world.

Her family was different. Her adoptive parents traveled all the time—but almost never took their children with them. They either had no relatives, or, for some reason, never mentioned or contacted them. Sometimes they would have deep conversations, but they always stopped talking when the children entered the room.

Mama and Daddy both seemed to have jobs—but would never let anyone know exactly what they were. "We work for the family business," she remembered her father saying, the first time she had asked.

"But what do you do?" she had persisted.

"It's complicated," Dad had replied. "I'll tell you when you're older."

That phrase, Miranda realized, summed up the answers to most of the questions she and Marko asked her parents. *When you're older.* From her earliest memories to now, she had been waiting for answers that never came.

Instead, everything deteriorated. Money became tighter. Smiles became fewer. Laughter disappeared altogether. Her parents spent more time on the road, and on the few occasions they were at home, they looked tired and defeated, and spent most of their time locked in the study, planning their next trip.

Since their parents were rarely home, and there was no money to pay for babysitters, Miranda and Marko spent most of their time with their grandfather in the old family house, the last building on a dead-end road in a suburb south of the city.

Grandfather, whom they called Ye Ye, was a historian with a practical turn of mind and the instincts of a collector. He would read about ancient objects or books—and then go out looking for them. He was absentminded, and often seemed more than a little crazy, but he loved them and they felt safe with him.

This summer, Mama and Daddy had not been back for weeks, and Ye Ye had taken their place. But now he was gone, too.

"We're cursed," Miranda had said out loud. "That's the only explanation."

Beep-beep-beep-beep. She had been snapped out of her gloom by a tiny bleating noise from her watch. It was time for her favorite television show. She went back indoors.

Miranda never allowed herself to feel downhearted for long. She was as adventurous as her brother was nervous, so she had decided to look on the bright side. There was no one to tell her what to eat, what to watch, and when to go to bed. Some kids dream of being in such a situation. She decided she would stay up watching television and eating marshmallows until she felt sleepy. At eleven o'clock she went to bed, falling asleep the moment her head touched her pillow.

And the following morning, she had stumbled into the dining room to see her brother emerging from the kitchen with dessert for breakfast. Clearly he, too, had decided to look on the bright side.

* * *

The two children passed their second day alone, playing with toys, reading, and just staring out of the window. They ate instant noodles or cereal when they were hungry.

But as the afternoon turned into evening, Marko's face became serious.

"Something's wrong," he said. "We shouldn't be on our own, should we?"

She put one hand on his shoulder. She wasn't usually affectionate with her brother, but she felt sorry for him. Marko was a quiet, shy boy and liked nothing better than to spend as much time as possible at home, surrounded by family members, and reading. He read so much and so fast that he usually carried a few books with him in a backpack—wherever he went, even at home, just so he'd never be caught without something to read. In a bid to help him be more sociable, Miranda had encouraged him to sign up for a variety of activities at school. But he had quickly dropped out of all the fashionable ones, like dancing and computers. The only thing he had been good at was the long jump, a rather obscure activity which was not something that made good conversation.

"When's Ye Ye coming back?" he asked for the umpteenth time.

"Soon, Marko, soon."

"How do you know?"

"Because Ye Ye is Ye Ye. He has amazing adventures on his trips. But he always comes back."

"But he never goes away when Mama and Dad are away."

"He's probably just lost track of time. You know how he gets caught up in things. He'll be … fine." She was aware of the lack of conviction in her voice.

Marko nodded half-heartedly.

Then Miranda remembered something that she thought might cheer him up. "Besides, Ye Ye promised to train you to win the long jump in the next junior games," she said. "And he always keeps his promises."

Marko managed half a smile.

Miranda opened her mouth to speak again, but was interrupted by the sound of the door knocker.

"Hey! Maybe that's him now."

Few people visited this house in a quiet back street in the leafier part of the coastal city of Hong Hai, so any activity at the front door was a major cause of excitement.

Their grandfather often arrived home from his travels carrying so much that he couldn't reach his key and would knock on the door, or just kick at it, to attract attention.

Marko reached the door first and wrenched it open. But the figure who stood there was not their grandfather. It was a tall stranger carrying a box.

"Special delivery for Mr. Lee," he said, holding out a receipt to be signed. Miranda scribbled on it.

Marko's eyes grew wide as he stared at the package. "Mira ... look at the handwriting," he said. "It's a box. From Ye Ye."

The Delivery

Normally the children would not open a package delivered to their grandfather, even if it looked large and exciting. They might shake it, examine the address label, or peer through any bits of torn wrapping, but they would wait until he got home before they opened it.

But this time was different. Grandfather had disappeared. He'd left no note. He hadn't called. There were no clues in his study about where he had gone or when he was returning. And if he didn't return soon, there would be trouble. They'd have to go and call the police or something. And Ye Ye would get into trouble for leaving them alone.

They needed to work out where he was and contact him. This package was not just an item of mail. It was a clue.

"There may be a return address or a phone number or a letter somewhere inside," Miranda said, suddenly breathless.

They tore off the brown paper wrapping and found a hinged box labeled "Mirror of the Moon." There was no letter in the package.

"Maybe there's a note inside the wooden box-thing," said Marko, undoing the latch and lifting the lid.

But there was no letter inside, either. The box contained nothing but some sort of old bronze plate. It was about the size of a serving dish, and the surface was dull and aged.

"Yuck," said Miranda. "It's just another bit of the old junk that Ye Ye likes to collect."

Marko agreed. He was as disappointed as she was.

"But at least it shows he's alive. That's got to be good news."

The boy nodded, semismiling for the first time that day. Then his eyes suddenly brightened. "You know what this is, don't you?" he said. "It's a magic mirror."

"Hmm?" Miranda thought Marko took Ye Ye's adventure stories much too seriously.

"Do you remember he told us about all those ancient treasure things from China? One was a magic mirror?"

She thought for a moment. "I think so. I remember it a bit. Let me see ..."

The two of them went through their grandfather's shelves. Most of the books were large, dusty, old hardbacks on history and antiques and travel, but there were a few that contained thought-provoking stories and legends, mostly about exploration, that he would read out loud to them.

Marko found the volume first. "Here." He held it up.

His big sister deftly plucked the book from his hands and flicked through the pages, quickly finding the chapter they were seeking. She read it out loud to her brother, although in truth, he was probably a better reader than she was.

"One of the most intriguing items from ancient China are the bronze artifacts known as magic mirrors. From one side, a magic mirror is simply a polished metal plate which can be used as a reflective surface. But if you hold it up to a source of illumination and the light passes through it, the markings on the other side are projected onto a wall or other surface. The projected images are said to have magical qualities."

She put down the book and her eyes turned to her grandfather's desk. "We can use his desk lamp to shine through it. See if it works. Maybe it will give us some sort of clue about where he is. Maybe that's what we are supposed to do. You know how Ye Ye likes to give us riddles and challenges."

Her brother picked up the bronze plate and turned it over. Strange lines and markings covered the entire back surface.

"Let me see that," she said.

"Mira! Don't snatch," he yelled, trying to grab it back.

"I just want to see," she said, holding it high, out of his reach. She was taller than her brother, and used the extra height to good effect. She turned it over and looked at the front. "It's too old and scratched to reflect any—hang on."

At first glance, the surface seemed to have lost its reflective qualities. But as she stared at it, she seemed to be able to make out the reflection of her eyes.

"I can see my eyes ... weird ... they look green."

"Lemme see."

"Just hang on."

The eyes in the mirror blinked.

Miranda was not aware of having blinked. She stared harder at the mirror, this time holding her eyes open as wide as possible.

The green eyes in the mirror stared back at her. Then they blinked again.

This time she was sure she had not blinked. That could only mean one thing: the eyes in the mirror were not her eyes!

"Aaaaah!" She gave a little shriek and dropped the mirror. It hit the floor with a clank and rolled toward her brother.

"You idiot. Why did you do that?" Marko bent to pick it up. "Good thing it's metal. It's seven years of bad luck to break a mirror, you know."

"The—the eyes I saw in the mirror. They weren't mine."

"What are you talking about?" She sat down without responding.

He held it up to his face, but the old, flat surface now seemed dead. There were no reflections of any kind on it.

Miranda bit the middle joint of her index finger.

"That was so weird. I thought I saw a pair of green eyes looking out at me. They blinked."

"Optical delusion."

"Illusion."

"Whatever."

She turned to see if there was anything behind her in the room that could have made that reflection.

There was nothing. She gave herself a little shake to compose herself. Then she reached over for the desk lamp. "Let's shine this through it. See if we can project an image on the wall."

"It won't work," Marko said.

"How do you know?"

"Look at the box. It says 'Mirror of the Moon.' We're going to need moonlight to shine through it."

"Where are we going to get some moonlight?"

Instinctively, they both turned to the round window on the east side of their grandfather's study.

Darkness was falling fast.

The Magic Mirror

Marko and Miranda Lee sat for more than an hour in their grandfather's study, leafing through old books, and looking at the darkening night sky.

It was a stormy, windy evening, and thick clouds scudded across a gray, swirling canopy. Although, according to the calendar on the desk, the moon was supposed to be full that night, it was almost invisible. All they could see was a slight glow to the east of the sky, lost behind thick layers of rainclouds.

It was a strange, rather spooky night. Gusts of wind picked up leaves and twigs and seemed to throw them in handfuls at the window. The sound gave Miranda the creeps. It sounded as if there was a witch outside, throwing things at the glass. Sometimes, she felt she had way too much imagination.

Marko looked up for the fiftieth time from the book he was reading (*Strange Sea Phenomena*) and sighed at the darkness outside. "There's not going to be any moonlight, tonight, is there, sis?"

She shook her head wearily. "Not tonight. Too cloudy."

He sighed. "I'm going to bed." He closed his book and put his hand up to his mouth, which opened as wide as a cat's to let out an enormous yawn.

Miranda rubbed her eyes. "Maybe tomorrow."

They left the study, closing the door behind them.

"I wish we had a normal family and a normal grandfather," said Marko. "Not one who always disappears on adventures."

"I know what you mean. But you know what Ye Ye always says ... 'The edge is where the action is.' He always wants to be at the cutting edge of every discovery, every bit of exploration. He's way more exciting than a normal, boring grandfather."

"Except when it means we don't have any grandfather at all."

"Yeah."

Halfway up the stairs, Marko stopped. "I think I'll take that book with me."

He went back downstairs and pulled open the study door. Seconds later, he was calling out to his sister. "Quick! Come look!"

Hearing the excitement in his voice, Miranda bolted down the staircase. Halfway down, she saw what Marko meant: Moonlight had turned the room silver-white. The light slanted diagonally through the windows and a glowing beam was focused right on the box containing the mirror.

The two children walked rapidly to the center of the room.

"Let me do it," said Miranda, opening the lid of the box.

"No. I want to hold it. It was my idea to come back."

"I'm older than you. I'm the boss in this house when Ye Ye's away."

"You're not the boss of me."

"Yes, I am."

They glared at each other over the mirror.

Then the moonlight from outside flickered and faded. It disappeared.

They both turned to the window and saw that a cloud had covered the moon. But the winds seemed to be blowing harder than ever. The clouds were racing across the sky at high speed. It was clear that there was a good chance there would be more moonlight before long.

"We'd better be ready when the light comes back," said Miranda. "Let's do it together."

Each holding one side of the magic mirror, they held it up and moved to the circular window, holding the slightly convex bronze plate as close as they could to the frame. They stood with their backs to the window, staring into the room.

The dark cloud obscuring the moon blew away and silver light flooded through the window—and through the magic mirror.

Miranda gasped. The room immediately brightened. But this time it was not the pale, dead light of the moon—nor was it their grandfather's furniture that was being illuminated.

The white light turned reddish-gold on its journey through the bronze mirror and the room was filled with unfamiliar lines and shapes in shades of yellow, crimson, and brown. The shapes seemed to glow and even shift as she watched. Miranda felt dizzy.

The light became brighter and brighter. This was not just moonlight. It was more like a floodlight. There was something magical about the mirror. It seemed to intensify the light.

"The room's moving," Marko breathed.

Miranda realized he was right. The walls seemed to be swaying, as if the whole house was tilting to one side. And then it paused for a moment and swayed the other way.

"It's swinging. Like a pendulum," she said.

The light became so dazzling that it started to hurt her eyes. Terrified, and starting to feel faint, she closed her eyes and dropped the mirror.

"Or a ship," she heard her brother say, as she fell to the ground.

On Board

Miranda sat on the floor, her eyes screwed tightly shut.

This was way too weird. She did not want to open her eyes until the searing light had gone away. She wanted to be back in her home, dark, empty, and grandfatherless though it might be.

Opening her eyelids just a sliver, she noted that the dazzling light had disappeared. The scary vision of the golden swaying room must have gone. She opened her eyes fully to look around, and gasped.

She was not in the study at home, but in a large, unfamiliar room, which was still ever-so-gently swaying from side to side—like the captain's cabin of an ocean liner. It was an old-fashioned, wood-paneled room, and ornate Chinese carvings framed the doorways and window frames.

"Marko."

"Yes."

"Where are we?"

"I don't know where you are. But I'm in the middle of this amazing dream. I'm dreaming that I'm in a big room in an old ship somewhere."

"Marko."

"Yes."

"I'm having the same dream."

They turned to look at each other.

"This is weird," Miranda said.

Her brother nodded. He tapped the floor with his index finger. "It's a really vivid dream. Really feels like wood."

"If it's a dream we should be able to wake up."

"True."

Instinctively, they both screwed up their eyes. "I'm

going to count to ten, and then we'll open our eyes and we'll wake up at home. OK?"

He nodded. "OK."

"One. Two. Three. Four. Five. Six. Seven. Eight. Nine. Ten."

They both opened their eyes. Miranda turned to her brother. "I'm still in the dream. You?"

"Yeah. Am I in your dream or are you in my dream?"

"You're in my dream."

He thought for a moment. "That's just how it seems to you. But actually, I think you're in my dream. We can compare when we wake up. Let's have a look around. This is kind of interesting."

The two children climbed to their feet. Miranda put the magic mirror into Marko's backpack. "We might as well explore for a while before we wake up," she said. "I've read about this sort of thing. It's called a lucid dream. Where everything seems really real, and you can touch things and feel their texture and everything."

"And even smell things," said Marko, sniffing.

"Yeah." She took a deep breath and her eyes widened. "Food. Next door." They moved toward the doorway and inhaled. From the next room came the unmistakable sweet, singed aroma of freshly barbecued meat.

Marko, cautious by nature, hated opening doors unless he knew exactly what was on the other side. He dropped back to let his older sister take the lead.

She turned the strange, old-fashioned handle as quietly as she could and put her eye to the crack.

"There's a whole, like, buffet thing laid out," she whispered. "And no one there to eat it."

She swung the door wide open to show him a large wooden table piled with food in a room lit only by the moonlight shining through a porthole.

They'd been living largely on instant noodles, sausages, and cereal since Ye Ye had disappeared, and the smell of freshly cooked meat drew them like flies to honey.

"Wow," the boy breathed.

"Wow squared."

They moved quickly to the table. Miranda scanned the dishes—a huge platter of roast pork, plates of fruit and vegetables, some sort of flat bread, and many other dishes she didn't recognize.

"This is like one of those huge breakfast buffets you get in hotels," said Marko. "I wonder if they have waffles?"

Miranda's gaze zeroed in on a dark, glazed head with a small fruit in its mouth at the far end of the table in the gloomy room. But the snout seemed all wrong. "That's not a pig's head. What is it?"

"A monkey's head?" offered Marko.

Miranda shook her head. "Too big. It looks like …"

She looked at the small nose and at the same time noticed the ears, which were clearly human. She didn't need to finish her sentence. Marko had obviously noticed the same thing at the same time. They turned to each other and screamed.

The blackened human head opened its mouth to scream, too—and once the fruit had fallen away, shrieked loudest of all.

Lin's Warning

A minute later, Miranda and Marko were back in the room in which they had first opened their eyes. The boy hid, trembling, behind his sister.

The blackened head, and the body which belonged to it, was peering at them through the doorway.

They could see now that it wasn't a disembodied, cooked head at all. It was a young woman, a little older and taller than Miranda. The girl was covered from head to toe in some sort of black, tarry oil. Beneath the dark coating she wore a ruined long tunic and loose trousers.

"I'm sorry," she said, in strangely accented Mandarin. "I didn't mean to scare you. I was just so hungry. I only took one fruit from your table."

"Stay away from us," Miranda yelped, keeping as much distance as possible between herself and the newcomer. She tried to keep her voice steady. "Who are you? And where are we? And how did we get here?"

"And how do we get back home?" added Marko from behind her.

The girl looked puzzled. She stepped into the room. "Don't come any closer, or … I'll … do … something," Miranda finished lamely. She turned to her brother. He pulled the magic mirror out of his backpack and handed it to her. She held it in front of her, ready to throw like a Frisbee.

"I won't hurt you," the girl said, holding up her open palms in a gesture of peace. "I need your help."

"You need our help?" asked Miranda. "Then we're all in trouble. We're stuck in a really weird dream. We need major work from psychologists or something."

"Who are you?" the girl asked. "I'll tell you who I am. My name's Shi Lin. They wouldn't let me on board, so I hid in a barrel half-full of oil and was carried in. But I've been hiding for hours. And I got so hungry…"

Miranda realized that the girl was as scared as she was, and lowered the bronze plate. "Got on board where? Where exactly are we?"

The girl looked puzzled. "You don't know? You don't belong here either? You also are stowaways?"

"I guess we are."

"Do you not even know whose ship this is?"

The two younger children shook their heads.

"So we're all in the same boat," said Marko. "That's a joke. Get it?"

"Come," the girl said, beckoning them back to the dining room. "We'll take some food—and then we'll find a safe place to talk."

But as she picked food off the table, carefully taking just one or two items from each plate so nothing would be missed, she spoke rapidly and nervously.

"I'm Shi Lin, daughter of Shi Jing-qing—you know who that is?"

Miranda shook her head. "No, we don't know anyone round here—we don't even know where 'here' is."

"How did you get here?"

Miranda and her brother looked at each other. "It's a long story," she said.

"Never mind. I will tell you my news. It's urgent. My father Shi Jing-qing is the Head of the Old Port— the one on the southern Chalk Coast, just above Crescent Moon Harbor. The Pirate King and his men have been attacking us for weeks. Chen Zuyi and his men—they're merciless killers."

A shudder ran through her body as she mentioned this name. "They burned our houses and stole everything. They robbed the ships and emptied the temples. They said that on their next visit they will kill every man, woman, and child who resists them."

"Pirates?" Marko asked. "Real pirates, like with swords and boats and stuff?"

"What other breed of pirate is there?"

"Never mind."

Miranda interrupted. "Whose ship is this? Is this your father's ship?"

"My father's ship has been sunk. But it was a small boat. Not like this ship, the greatest sea vessel ever made. Can it be that you really don't know where you are?"

Seeing the blankness on Miranda's face, Lin continued, "You two know as little as newborns! We're stowaways on the leading vessel of the fleet of Admiral Zheng He."

"Jen who?" asked Miranda.

"Admiral Zheng He," said Lin.

Marko brightened. "We did a project about him. He was a famous sailor. He lived in the 1400s, I think."

Lin ignored him and continued, "Admiral Zheng He is the greatest seaman in China—probably the bravest explorer alive, anywhere in the world. He's been to the lands beyond the seas, they say."

"Meaning what? Australia? America?" This was Marko.

"Is he on your side?" Miranda asked.

"He is on his own side," Lin replied. "The Admiral is a hard man. And a busy one with great responsibilities for the Emperor. But my father was informed by secret messenger two days ago that the Admiral's fleet was going to be in the seas close to us. We realized that he must be on his way to fight the Pirate King."

She suddenly looked downcast. "But two days ago the pirates attacked again. They killed many of my countrymen and boasted that they were going to ambush the Admiral. Somehow the Pirate King knew all about the arrival of the fleet."

"I guess the Pirate King has spies," said Miranda.

Lin nodded. "I knew I had to warn him, so I traveled many miles on a fishing boat. And then I reached a harbor where this fleet arrived to take on food and fuel. But no one would listen to me. No one would take my message seriously. So I hid in an oil barrel and was carried on board."

She stopped and turned her head. They heard heavy footsteps and male voices. A group of men were approaching the outer door that led to the dining room.

The three children raced in the opposite direction, to the door that led to the inner cabin.

But before Marko's hand reached the handle, both doors burst open.

The youngsters shrieked.

A large, heavily armed man stood blocking the doorway in front of them.

"Well, well, well," he said, pulling out his sword. "What have we here? Rats nibbling at our dinner? Time to do a bit of pest killing, I think."

Prisoners

The three children were tied together with coarse rope and led by guards along endless gloomy, creaking corridors. Then, they were forced down a swaying staircase. It was clear where they were being taken: the ship's dungeons, the brig.

"We don't belong here," Miranda pleaded. "We need to get home. You need to let us go. Please."

The guard in front turned to glare at her. "We'll let you go, all right. We'll let you go to the ship's deepest, darkest brig ... if you're lucky."

The guard walking behind them, a younger man, gave a short, sharp laugh. "He's right. The lucky ones get locked away. Most stowaways are thrown overboard Snack time for sharks."

His comments scared Miranda into shocked silence.

Lin spoke up. "My name's Shi Lin. I'm the daughter of Shi Jing-qing, Head of Old Port. I have a seal, look."

She raised her right hand to show a large red-surfaced ring on her finger.

"Copied or stolen," growled the guard.

"It's real," the girl replied. "Please believe me. I've got an urgent message for Admiral Zheng He. I must give it to him."

The old guard in front turned and glared at her with angry eyes. "You are a filthy stowaway and will never utter that name again, if you want to live."

"Please," she said, bowing her head. "I don't mean any disrespect. I know your commander is Lord of the Western Seas. But I'm telling the truth. I have information for him—important information."

"Tell it to the brig walls."

"Please, if you can get a message to my father, he will tell—"

"You don't look like the daughter of a chief, covered in filth," the guard said. He tried to sound scornful, but his voice had softened, and there was a trace of curiosity in his eyes.

"I hid in a barrel of oil to get on board—and before that, I was in hiding in a place that was attacked by a very dangerous man named Chen Zuyi."

The older guard stopped dead in his tracks. He turned around and stared at Lin. She had caught his attention.

She spoke quickly, "Yes, I know about Chen Zuyi. I was with the Pirate King two days ago—hidden not fifty steps away from him. And I know you're heading towards the Mu Si estuary. But I'm here to warn you— you're heading into a trap. Chen knows you're coming. His most dangerous vessels are hidden away. He's got a plan to corner you and destroy your fleet."

The younger guard behind them spoke up. "If you're really the daughter of the harbormaster of Old Port, tell us: What is the region called on the maps?"

"Palembang."

"What do the locals call it?"

"The locals call it Gaw Gong, but the northern sailors say Jiu Gang."

"Where is Chen Zuyi from?"

"He is a criminal from Teochew."

"What are the titles of the Admiral?"

"Lord of the Western Seas, Master of the Oceans, Helmsman of the Treasure Fleet, Commander of the Sea Dragons ... shall I go on?"

He stared at her curiously. "And you say Chen Zuyi has set a trap for us?"

"Yes. He knows you're on your way and he's going to ambush you."

The two guards stared at each other over the heads of their three prisoners.

The older guard wrinkled his nose and looked skeptical. "They're just kids. What could they know?"

His companion looked worried. "What if she's telling the truth?"

"It's not possible. Come on, we're wasting time."

He pulled at the rope, and the small, unhappy expedition continued on its journey toward the bowels of the ship.

But then the corridor behind them was filled with the sound of running footsteps.

A voice called out. "Stop. On the orders of the Supreme Commander."

A breathless sailor caught up with them.

"What is it?" the rear guard asked.

"The Admiral wants you to head up to the Chart Room now."

The older guard looked nervous. "What does he want to see us for?"

The sailor shook his head. "He doesn't want to see you. He wants to see them." He nodded at the children.

The Chart Room

Miranda, Marko, and Shi Lin were taken up the stairs and ushered into a large room, where they were completely ignored by several large men who were standing around a table looking at maps.

"That's him," whispered Lin to Miranda. The young girl followed the stowaway's gaze and realized that she was staring at an unusually tall man, dressed in regal armor and flowing robes of golden silk. Clearly he belonged to some sort of royal court.

"Yao Ming?" whispered Marko, noticing the man's unusual height.

"Shh," hissed his sister.

The guard escorting them coughed to get the commander's attention. "My Lord, I have brought the stowaways as you requested."

The Admiral turned around and gave the newcomers the briefest of glances before returning his attention to the map. "Put them in my office," he growled in a voice as low as the rumble of thunder. "I'll speak to them later."

Miranda stared at his face. He did not appear to have what she thought of as Chinese features. He looked like a member of one of China's minority tribes. He had a squareish face with round eyes, a prominent nose, and nut-brown skin. His cheeks were rough and pockmarked, and he had intense dark eyes under heavy eyelashes and thick eyebrows.

The guard prodded Miranda, forcing her to move away. They were ushered into a cabin and told to stand and wait.

The Admiral entered a few minutes later, bending his huge frame to get through the doorway. His voice was stern and his words curt.

"We are in a war situation," he said. "People who stow away during a time of battle are assumed to be spies. The punishment for spying is death. There are no exceptions."

"Please," said Miranda. "Marko and I … we're just looking for our grandfather. He's all we've got and we've lost him. We're really not—"

"Silence," the guard shouted. "You speak only when the Admiral asks you a question."

Ignoring him, Lin poured out her story. "I'm Shi Lin, daughter of Shi Jing-qing, Master of Old Port in Palembang, Malacca. He sent me with a message: Chen Zuyi is going to ambush your fleet. You must find another route."

The Admiral turned to look at her. He raised his eyebrows slightly, his expression inviting her to continue.

"It's true. My father sent me to warn you. I know who you are. You are Admiral Zheng He, the one they call the Lord of the Western Seas, Master of the Oceans, Helmsman of the Treasure Fleet. My father knows you. And even I met you once before, when I was a small child." She fell to her knees and bowed her head in respect.

The Admiral's stern expression softened slightly. "To me, you are still a small child," he said quietly.

He walked two steps closer and peered at her. She lifted her head and looked him in the eye.

The Admiral tilted his head to one side and spoke slowly, recalling a distant memory. "Palembang, eh? I visited your father, once—several years ago. I remember seeing a small girl on his wife's hip. You?"

Lin bowed her head again. "I am your servant."

"You have information?"

"The Pirate King came to our land and killed many people. You are his next target."

He nodded slowly. "I'll send someone to take you and your companions to be fed and housed. If you genuinely have useful information about Chen's plans, then we can use you."

Miranda put her hand up, as if she was asking a question at school. "Please, sir," she said. "Thank you for sparing us, but … can I ask you … why did you ask to see us … instead of locking us up or throwing us overboard—"

He turned to face her. "It's a reasonable question and deserves a fair answer."

He sat down, bringing his face to the same height as hers, and spoke more gently. "My father was a sailor, and his father before him. They had many great adventures, some extremely dangerous. Sometimes I would go with them. But when I was eleven years old, I was captured. I was wounded, badly, by my captors, but I survived."

He looked out of the window for a moment, and his eyes narrowed, as if he was reliving a deeply painful memory.

"It is hard for a child to bear such fear and such pain, especially alone. When my men informed me that child stowaways had been captured on this ship, I was reminded of the terror I felt at that time. If I had let them harm you, I would have been as bad as the men who harmed me. And that is something I could not allow."

He stood up and marched out of the room.

* * *

Half an hour later, the three children were again taken into the Chart Room. Scrubbed clean and dressed in clean clothes, Shi Lin looked transformed: now she was every inch the tall, proud daughter of a local nobleman. She marched straight over to the map table.

In the interim, the Admiral's men had been joined by a thin, wiry man in robes of expensive blue silk. He turned and faced the young woman as she approached.

As she caught sight of his face, Shi Lin froze to the spot. Her face had an expression that revealed a combination of fear, suspicion, and disgust.

Apparently not noticing this, Admiral Zheng He briefly introduced her to the men around the table. A small brown man to his left was Yusof, the ship's navigator. Then there was a man with an Italian-sounding name which she could not quite catch. The Admiral then pointed to the sharp-faced man in blue silk. "And this—"

"I know who that is," Lin said.

"Liang Dao Ming," said the man in blue. "At the Admiral's service." He bowed, directing his eyes not at her, but at his commander.

Lin, clearly unnerved by his presence, moved to the side of the table as far from him as possible. Miranda noticed that she was blinking rapidly.

The girl from Old Port bent over the map. "See this harbor opening here?" Her finger hovered over an estuary shaped like a vase.

Miranda, peering from a distance, noticed that the inlet at which she was pointing had a narrow neck leading from the open sea to a slightly wider area of inland water, which then turned into a river. The main body of water was fed by numerous smaller streams and watercourses.

"That's where the trap is," Shi Lin said.

The Admiral nodded. "It is perfectly designed for an ambush," he said. "We sail through the narrow opening, into the inland waters. Then they block our retreat and attack from all sides. There'll be nowhere we can turn."

Liang Dao Ming laced his fingers together. "It would be a battle we cannot win," he said in a grating, raspy voice. "We must turn back. We must regroup and draw the pirates away, to the open sea."

The Admiral shook his head. "No. We continue straight ahead. We are going to go for the battle, right there on the coast. And we are going to win."

The Treasure Ship

L et's go outside," Marko whispered.

Without waiting for an answer from his sister, he stepped toward a large pair of double doors and pushed at it. But they were too heavy for him.

Miranda wasn't sure what to do. She glanced back at the center of the room, where Shi Lin and the men were lost in their maps and strategies of warfare.

"OK, let's have a quick look," she told her brother, helping him push. As the doors started to swing backward, dazzling white sunlight streamed through the gap. Half closing their eyes, Miranda and Marko slid through the part-opened door and stood on the outer veranda of the deck.

The sight that caught their eyes was breathtaking.

They were on a huge ship, longer than any vessel they had ever seen. The deck seemed to stretch into the far distance, giving the illusion of being an island. It had multiple levels—and most of them were packed with people scurrying around, carrying objects, calling to each other, and even buying and selling things.

And the vessel wasn't just large. It was elegant and regal, like a majestic floating palace. The pillars and cornices were ornate, and the railings were carved into snake and dragon shapes.

And then there were the masts. They had seen boats with traditional Chinese "batwing" masts many times, but each vessel usually had a single midsized sail, and perhaps one or two much smaller ones. In contrast, Zheng He's massive ship had nine huge sails standing as tall as ancient forest trees, each carrying several huge batwing sails.

"This ship is amazing," breathed Miranda. "It's as big as an aircraft carrier."

There was no reply. She turned around to speak to her brother but he had vanished.

"Marko?"

"I'm up here. Come and see this. You are so not going to believe this."

He had climbed up a small staircase to a balcony above the Chart Room, and was gazing to the rear of the ship.

His sister scrambled up beside him to see what had caught his attention. What she saw took her breath away.

There was not just one massive ship in this part of the sea. There was a whole fleet of them. Following behind Admiral Zheng He's huge vessel were hundreds of others. It was a huge, floating city, stretching all the way to the horizon. Large numbers of rust-red masts formed a moving, undulating forest pointing to the sky.

"Wow. What are all these ships?" Miranda asked. "Is it like an armada or something?"

"I can answer that," said a voice. A young man was striding confidently up the steps she had just climbed. He was tall and thin, and wore a small round cap, a shiny red shirt, and baggy black trousers tied high about his ankles. He grinned, showing a gold tooth.

"I am Yung Qui," he said. "The Commander asked me to be your host. I will answer any questions you have, honored visitors."

Miranda pointed to the huge fleet behind them. "This ship is huge. Are all these ships the same as this one?"

"Certainly not. This is a floating kingdom, and every part of it has its own tasks and specialties. Some call it Sea Dragon City," he said. "There are 300 ships in the fleet, and every unit has its purpose. Some are battleships. Some carry soldiers."

As he spoke, he pointed to different groups of ships. "Look! There are cavalry ships stabling horses. Over here are attack ships, which move fast and stay low in the water. There to the east are supply ships, and there to the west are freshwater ferries, which we use to collect water supplies from the coast."

He spoke quickly. It was evident that he had given this speech many times before.

Miranda looked him up and down. Despite his funny clothes and odd accent, the boy had style, she decided. He was confident, self-assured, and acted as if he knew everything about everything. If they'd really gone back in time to the 1400s, he was quite possibly one of the world's first professional tour guides, she mused.

The boy continued, "Note the dragon's eye painted on the side of each ship. We are known as the Fleet of Sea Dragons, the most powerful convoy of ships in history."

"You must have a lot of sailors to drive all these ships," she said.

"You don't drive ships," Marko said. "You man them."

"That sounds sexist to me," Miranda sneered.

"We have many sailors," their guide interrupted. "But we also have people of all other professions. We have doctors, astronomers, priests, musicians, and many others. There are 27,800 souls on board the Sea Dragon fleet—almost 1,000 on each ship. And of course, we have our cargo of treasure."

* * *

Yung Qui turned out to be the perfect host.

Over the next three days, he took them all over the ship, and they even made brief visits to a few of the other vessels, crossing from one to the other on rickety string-and-wood bridges slung between them.

Miranda was fascinated by the storerooms of treasure with which the ships were loaded: gold and silver ware, beautiful silks and linen, and delicate porcelain, mostly in blue and white.

She was intrigued to learn that the treasures were not items stolen from other lands to take back to the royal court, but had been loaded on board from the king's house, to give as gifts to strangers.

"That is so weird," she said. "You guys are like reverse pirates. You go around giving treasure away to people you don't know."

Marko was too shy to speak to Yung Qui at first, but he soon opened up. Fired by his natural curiosity, he satisfied his thirst for information by exploring the ships and questioning their guide.

Miranda realized that her brother must feel as if he had managed to climb right inside one of the history textbooks that he so loved.

Marko was particularly fascinated by the unusual and rare substances on board. There were many casks of spices, each of which had its own powerful scent. He was intrigued by a type of wood called camphor, which gave off a powerful, soothing odor: It reminded him of being a baby, he told his sister. Their mother must have used it.

And then there was a storeroom full of something which Yung Qui described as "black gold."

"How can gold be black?" Miranda asked.

Yung Qui dipped his finger into a small, open keg and pulled out something like a small black seed. He raised his hand to her face and crushed it.

She immediately sneezed.

Marko laughed. "It's pepper," he said.

Days at Sea

The fleet traveled slowly, but there was a lot of work to be done. And everybody had to do their share—including Miranda and Marko.

Cannons had to be cleaned and primed, ammunition had to be prepared, and there was lots of below-deck work for the youngsters in the catering and provisions department, too. The Sea Dragon fleet had a huge range of provisions to feed its large population, and there were endless mountains of vegetables to be cut and bowls to be washed. The youngsters, although they were assumed to be noblemen's children from foreign lands, were happy to join in with the work.

Caught up in the all-day blur of activity, their worries about searching for their grandfather and being so far from home were pushed to the back of their minds. The salty air seemed to give them energy that they enjoyed expending. They went to sleep every night exhausted.

On the fourth day of the voyage, Yung Qui and Shi Lin joined them for a late meal in a cabin near the front of the ship. The four of them swapped stories about the amazing things they had seen in their lives.

"On one voyage last year, we saw a mountain spouting fire," said Qui.

"We know about those. We call them volcanoes," said Miranda, her competitive streak coming to the fore.

"We saw a black tiger with eyes burning red in the moonlight," the guide added.

"We call those black panthers."

"We counted a hundred islands around Sumatra alone."

"Have you been to Hong Kong? There are more than 200 islands there, and Indonesia and the Philippines have thousands of islands."

Shi Lin said, "I have not traveled far, but I have seen

many ships, and people from all over the world. I saw a man with yellow hair once, and a woman with green eyes."

"We have those where we come from," said Miranda. "And there's a girl in my class with purple hair. She thinks she looks cool but she doesn't. And she's got these little faces on her fingernails."

Shi Lin looked baffled, not knowing whether to take this information seriously or not.

In turn, Miranda and Marko tried to explain the wonders of their age to Yung Qui and Shi Lin. It wasn't easy.

"We have this thing called TV," said Miranda. "It's like a box with moving pictures."

"You mean paintings?" Qui asked.

"No, more like photographs," Marko said.

"What's a photograph?"

"Er, well, it's like a painting, sort of," he said.

"And we have planes," Miranda said. "Like ships that can fly. You can get hundreds of people inside, and they serve dinner in the air above the clouds. They're really cool."

Lin and Qui nodded politely, but she could tell from their eyes that they didn't believe her.

Miranda asked Shi Lin why she so disliked the man in blue silk.

"His name is Liang Dao Ming," she explained. "He is a chieftain who is based near the Old Port. He and my father are not friends. He cannot be trusted. We believe he wants to kill my father and all our family so he can be the King of Palembang."

"If he's a bad man, how come he's helping the Admiral?" Miranda asked.

"Bad men often get themselves into positions of power," she replied. "If your conscience is so weak that you have the ability to tell lies with a straight face, you can be anything to anyone."

Suddenly, there was a cry from the lookout tower.

Qui sprang to his feet.

"What is it?" Miranda asked.

"We've arrived."

They sprang out of the room and raced to the railings, staring at the horizon. For several minutes, they saw nothing but the rolling hills of the wide blue ocean. And then a tiny line appeared on the horizon. They had reached landfall.

They had arrived at the Lair of the Pirate King.

* * *

There was tension in the air as the convoy's lead vessel, known as the Treasure Ship, led the way through the narrow mouth of the bay. Within half an hour, they were floating slowly down the Mu Si River—site of the ambush Lin had warned them about.

Rain started to fall, making a thrumming noise on the wooden roof of the ship.

"The old sailors say a massive storm is brewing," Yung Qui reported, swapping his small cloth cap for a weather-beaten leather hat. "It could make things difficult on both sides."

Crouched underneath a wooden overhang, Miranda and Marko peered anxiously through a curtain of monsoon rain at the thick undergrowth masking the riverbank on both sides of the ship. Were there pirates there, waiting to board their ship and attack?

Miranda noticed a movement behind a tall, curved palm tree. "There! Look. I think I saw a man. Maybe one of the ambushers."

"You saw one man?" said Shi Lin. "I can see five men in that group of trees. And there are more than fifteen in those bushes over there."

Marko, shivering with fear, turned to her. "This is the ambush that you warned the Admiral about?"

She nodded.

"We're going straight into it, aren't we?"

She nodded again.

"You said the Pirate King planned to attack from the front and at the same time cut off our retreat. And then kill us all."

She nodded a third time.

Marko shook his head in bafflement. "If you warned him about this ambush, why are we sailing right into it?"

Lin did not answer.

Qui said, "The Helmsman has his own way of doing things. Sometimes we cannot see what his plans are, but we must trust him."

Miranda pointed to the shore. "I can see another man hiding on the shore."

Lin said, "And I can see another twenty."

The girl from Palembang turned to Marko and took his hand in hers. "Don't be scared, little boy. We must trust. That's all we can do."

The rain fell harder, and it became too noisy to speak.

The Ambush

As darkness fell, Miranda found herself feeling increasingly uncomfortable. What on earth were they doing here? Was this some sort of crazy dream? If so, when would they wake up? And if not, what had happened to them? Had they really gone back in time?

She realized that she had no way of finding the answers to all these questions. Their only hope lay in being able to find their grandfather. He would sort it all out for them. "Oh, Ye Ye," she said out loud to no one in particular. "Where are you? Are you looking for us? Are we going to find you? If we can't find each other, who's going to look after us? Who's going to save us?"

Over the next half hour, the rain stopped falling, but was replaced with a violent wind that came in short bursts, making the sails fill suddenly with curious cracking sounds, like gunfire.

Miranda heard a footstep behind her and realized that her brother was approaching. She took a deep breath and tried to banish the fear from her face.

"Well, this is a mighty big adventure, little bro," she said. "It'll be something to talk about at playtime when we get back to school. Not many kids have faced real pirates."

"Are pirates skeletons?" he asked, standing very close to her. "Can they be killed?"

"They're only skeletons sometimes in the movies," she replied. "These ones will be normal humans, I think."

The adults clearly felt the fear in the air, too. Few of the crew members spoke to the children or to each other. Instead, they worked in efficient silence, each one concentrating his energy on the task at hand.

Except for those posted as lookouts, the sailors seemed reluctant to even lift their eyes and acknowledge that anything existed beyond the boundaries of their floating world.

Looking over the railing toward the stern of the vessel, Miranda realized there were now some thirty ships from

Zheng He's fleet in a narrow line following the river.

And she shivered, realizing that there were probably 10,000 murderous pairs of eyes watching them from the trees on either side of the river.

Yung Qui emerged from the Chart Room and hurried over to them, his face grim.

"Follow me, now," he barked, immediately spinning on his heels and striding away.

"Where are we going?" Miranda asked, grabbing her brother's arm and pulling him along.

Qui did not turn or reply. His mind seemed elsewhere. The two youngsters had to almost run to keep up with his long legs. He strode purposefully to the rear of the boat, port side, and then led them down a staircase leading to a balcony area cut into the side of the boat. There were other children waiting there, plus several women with babies.

Another sailor arrived escorting a group of young women, which included Shi Lin.

"This is a transfer station," said Qui. "Wait here until a boat arrives to take you."

"Where are we being taken?" asked Lin.

"The Admiral has ordered that children and nursing women be taken off this ship and moved to the *Sparrow*. It's a small boat that will be anchored between the tail of this ship, on the port side, and the head of the second ship, on the starboard. You will be safer there, protected on both sides."

"But I want to stay and fight," said Shi Lin.

Qui turned without answering and raced back to his post.

* * *

Shortly afterward, the three young people found themselves transferred onto the good ship *Sparrow*, a small vessel neatly protected on each side by larger boats—the prow of one and the stern of the other.

Miranda noticed that her brother was shaking, even though the evening was warm. Although he annoyed her much of the time, there had been several times recently when she felt sorry for him. Poor Marko—he was such a nervous soul. It must be so difficult to go through life being scared all the time. And with Mama, Daddy, and Grandfather all disappearing as they seemed to have, it was not surprising he was so scared. What was there in his life which was stable? Nothing. He had no one left to depend on, except his big sister, and she was often so mean to him.

"Don't worry, Marko," she said, putting her arm around his shoulders. "Qui said we'd be safe here."

The young boy shook his head. "No. He said we'd be safer. That's not the same as safe. It might just mean that we'll be boarded by pirates in two hours, instead of one."

Miranda wondered what she could do to comfort him. She looked up at the large ship beside them.

"Look." There was some activity in the Treasure Ship's bridge area, which they could just see from their vantage point on the smaller ship.

Admiral Zheng He emerged from the Chart Room and climbed calmly to the top deck of the ship. In front of him was a huge drum on a raised podium.

He lifted a large and heavy hammer.

"He's going to beat that drum thing?" Miranda asked Shi Lin. "Will that be the sign for the fighting to start?"

"That's a thunder drum," she replied. "It can be heard for miles. It'll be a signal for his men to start fighting."

"What if the pirates start fighting first?"

Just then, they heard shouting. Something bright like a shooting star sparkled low in the evening sky.

"They have started," said Lin. "That's a fire lance."

The flame flew through the sky, arcing through the air toward the Treasure Ship.

"Look there," said Marko, pointing ahead of them.

The sun had dipped below the horizon, turning both sea and sky black. But Miranda could just make out that there was now a large pirate ship, black on black, visible directly ahead of them. Others seemed to be manifesting themselves from the dark shadows behind it.

The Admiral stood impassive, apparently waiting for the right moment to sound the drum and start the battle.

Miranda's fist flew to her mouth. She felt panic surging through her body, but tried to remain calm for the sake of her brother. All her senses came alive, and she felt supersensitive. She heard screamed orders in the far distance, and then there was the unmistakable shrill blast of some sort of trumpet shell from the shore. She could smell the burning wood from the flaming lances being hurled by their enemies. And she could detect thousands of tiny movements in the forests on either side of the river as the pirates prepared for battle.

Suddenly, flashes of light burst from the pirates' lead ship ahead of them. The explosions appeared in several different places at once, signifying that cannons had been fired. Seconds later, the rumbling of the cannons reached them. Then they heard a series of sickening crunching sounds as cannonballs slammed into the Treasure Ship. Everyone was yelling, the fear in their voices being carried over the water.

"They're shooting us," she said.

"You'd better get under cover," Lin ordered.

Miranda grabbed Marko and they moved backward toward the cabin area of the *Sparrow*, but she didn't enter, choosing instead to hover in the doorway. "If the ship catches fire, we don't want to be in a wooden room," she told Lin. "Besides I think we're better off seeing what's happening."

She looked up to the Treasure Ship, where the Admiral stood. He remained motionless, poised above the drum, with his hands in the air, clutching the huge hammer.

The coastal jungle on both sides of the river lit up as if strings of decorative lights had been turned on— but she knew they were flames that had been lit to use against their ships. Within minutes, the sky was filled with cascades of cannonballs and fire lances.

A heavy object soared through the air less than six feet in front of her and slammed into the floor of the *Sparrow*, smashing the timbers and disappearing below the deck.

Then a fire lance hit the wall of the cabin near where they stood. Lin jumped up and stamped the flames out with her leather-wrapped feet.

In the great vessel next to them, the Admiral remained motionless in front of the thunder drum.

"Look there," said Lin, pointing to the surface of the sea. Miranda ran to the railings to look down. Now they could see large, square platforms of flame in the inky water, moving outward from the riverbanks.

"They're pushing fire rafts into the river," Lin said. "The current will bring them straight to the Treasure Ship."

A group of men raced to the sides of the massive vessel and used long rods to keep the burning rafts from setting the Treasure Ship alight.

Marko closed his eyes tight and clapped his hands over his ears.

"Why doesn't he do something?" Miranda screamed as a new barrage of flying, burning spears flew toward the ships. "Why aren't we fighting back?"

The Admiral remained in place, unmoving as a statue. Not one weapon had yet been fired from the Treasure Ship.

A massive catapult-launched fire stick hit one of the masts of the great ship. In the brightening, flame-lit night, Miranda saw a long line of pirate ships now ranged straight ahead of them—there must have been fifteen or more.

And behind them, more pirate ships emerged from the darkness, blocking the only exit.

They were surrounded, just as Shi Lin had predicted. It could only mean one thing: certain death.

The Battle

L ook," Lin pointed at their leader.

Slowly, Admiral Zheng He lifted his hands.

When the hammer was far above his head, he brought it down sharply, and the thud that came from the drum shook the ship and reverberated across the water in all directions.

Miranda's hands flew to her ears. "Now I see why they call it the thunder drum," she said.

Seconds later, another rumble of flying cannonballs could be heard, and flames erupted all around them, but this time, the sounds appeared to come from a much greater distance.

Lin, who was watching the action carefully, looked confused—and then thrilled. She turned to Miranda and Marko. "The attacks are coming from behind the pirates," she said.

"Behind?" Marko asked.

"Yes," said Lin. "They're from people on our side. The Admiral had a plan. I knew he did."

* * *

As the battle raged all night, it became clear to Miranda why the Treasure Fleet had traveled so slowly to its destination at the mouth of the Mu Si River.

The Admiral had deliberately delayed the start of the battle so that his smaller, fast-moving attack boats could get into position. They had sped ahead and secretly taken positions in the smaller rivers and inlets that fed the river.

There they had waited, in darkness and silence—until they heard the unmistakable sound of the thunder drum: the signal that told them the Pirate King's fleet had turned itself into a group of sitting ducks, in an ideal position to be attacked from behind and on all sides.

The Treasure Ship had made itself the bait, and drawn the pirates into the center of the battle arena.

And now an unfair fight had become a fair one.

As the night wore on, many of the pirate fleet's ships became silent.

"Are we winning?" Miranda asked, peering out from the doorway where she and Marko had taken shelter.

Lin shook her head. "It's too early to say. They've lost some ships. We've lost some, too."

Although the Admiral's ship was intact, the vessel on the *Sparrow*'s starboard side had gone, moving to another part of the water where reinforcements had been needed.

"But every thing's gone quiet. Might that not mean we've won?"

"You don't know Chen Zuyi," Lin said. "The Pirate King is totally unpredictable."

Suddenly, there was a huge crash and the three children were thrown to the ground. The *Sparrow* had been violently rammed. They heard the sound of wood being crushed and splintered.

Miranda scrambled to her knees and looked to starboard as the boat rocked violently. A black painted ship, the same size as the *Sparrow*, had silently approached from the west and slammed hard into them. As she continued to stare, faces appeared from the side of the attackers' boat: cruel faces with long hair tied with dirty red scarves … the faces of pirates.

One man stood taller than the others. He held a cutlass. He had no hair on the top of his head, but long, straggly mustaches ran down each side of his mouth. His teeth were brown and crooked. He had a short, pointed beard.

To her left, she heard a gasp from Shi Lin. Miranda realized that this terrifying figure could only be one man: Chen Zuyi himself.

"Board her," the Pirate King screamed.

The pirates started to climb onto the *Sparrow*. Several of them wrapped thick ropes between the railings of the two boats, to bind them together.

Lin spoke in a voice dry with fear, "As I was saying, the Pirate King is totally unpredictable."

* * *

The pirates streamed over the railing onto the *Sparrow* and started grabbing everything they could. Barrels of water, bags of provisions, clothes, silks, and spare sails—anything that wasn't nailed in place was picked up to be transferred to their boat.

Lin suddenly got to her feet and marched straight towards the Pirate King. "Stop. You stop. This is a sanctuary boat," she hollered. "For children and women during battle. You cannot attack us. That's the rule of the sea."

The Pirate King turned to her. "What do we have here? A brave little mite of some sort? Well, let me tell you, little girl: This is my sea. I make the rules around here. And I break them, too, whenever I wish. Understood?"

She said nothing.

Suddenly losing his temper, he raised his cutlass and screamed at her at the top of his voice, "Understood?"

"Yes," she whimpered, backing away.

There was fresh blood visible on the blade of his knife.

The pirates herded the women and children to the front of the boat and then went through their belongings. They roughly grabbed purses, jewelry, necklaces, and rings.

One large pirate wrenched the backpack from Marko's shoulders and yanked it open, destroying the zipper. He stared inside. The magic mirror glinted. "Hidden treasure," he said. "Nice." He threw the bag onto the pile of items to be transferred to the pirate ship.

Within minutes, the intruders had gathered large piles of booty, which they then began flinging over the railings to their own ship. The operation was swift and efficient, perfected over years of plundering.

"Back," shouted the Pirate King, and they scrambled away over the railings.

Miranda watched horrified as the ropes tying the two boats together were untied.

The ropes became slack and the vessels started to drift apart.

"He's taken the magic mirror," she said quietly, her voice dull and flat.

Marko spoke like an echo, "He's taken the magic mirror."

They turned to face each other.

"Now we can never go back," she added.

"We're trapped here forever," Marko said. "Forever and ever. Amen."

The two children stood and watched in horror as

the pirate ship started to drift away, taking with it their only chance of ever returning home.

* * *

Miranda heard a high-pitched scream.

At first, she did not understand where it came from—and then realized it had come from the throat of her brother.

Marko shrieked his pain and anger out loud, and then started to run.

"What? Where are you—Marko! Stop!"

He raced directly toward the side of the ship.

She watched, her fist to her mouth, as he sprinted like a cheetah. And then she suddenly realized what he was doing: He was doing his long-jump run.

"No," she shouted. "It's too far. You'll never—"

But he could not be stopped. He raced like the wind to the side of the ship and hurled himself into the air. The gap between the two ships was already ten to thirteen feet wide and was increasing every second. He'd never make it.

Little Marko, his small legs bicycling in the air,

soared through space. Miranda was torn between her need to watch this tragedy unfold and the desire to close her eyes and pretend none of this was happening. Everything moved in slow motion. Inch by inch, Marko moved through the air—and somehow, miraculously, a powerful gust of wind from the approaching storm slammed him from behind, giving him the propulsion he needed to reach the pirate ship. He landed precariously on its railing. There was a heart-in-the-mouth moment where he was unbalanced, and could have fallen backward into the sea, but somehow he righted himself and fell forward, instead.

He flopped down ungracefully onto the deck of the pirates' ship.

Chen Zuyi had been marching toward his cabin, but his attention had been caught by Marko's unexpected arrival. He turned and stared at the small boy sitting in a breathless heap on the floor.

"Another brave little mite," he said. "So. You want to join us, do you?"

"That's mine," Marko said, pointing to the red backpack. "And I want it back."

The Pirate King tugged at his straggly whiskers without replying. Then he smiled—a grin filled with pure wickedness.

He grabbed the bag and lifted it over his head with

one hand. With his other hand, he reached for the long, sharp cutlass glinting by his belt. "Here it is. Come and get it, little flying boy."

"No," shouted Miranda. "He's got a sword. Marko! Leave it!"

Marko clambered to his feet, his face stony with determination, and ran straight toward Chen Zuyi.

But as the boy reached him, the Pirate King flung the bag away. It flew over the side of the boat, into the black sea. In the same swift movement, Chen drew out his bloody cutlass.

Marko spun to the right and threw himself off the edge of the boat. He disappeared into the impenetrable darkness of the midnight sea.

Miranda heard the splash of her brother hitting the water and she screamed.

Battle's End

She spun around, frantic and desperate. She grabbed Shi Lin by the shoulders. "My brother's in the water! We have to get help. Please, PLEASE!"

The young woman moved toward the railings to have a look. Miranda's eyes were suddenly full of frenzied tears. "He'll die! We have to help him."

Miranda turned around again and scanned the deck, looking for adults. One of the women, carrying a baby, stepped toward her. "My brother's in the sea. We need to save him," Miranda cried.

The woman handed the baby to a young girl behind

her and came to join Miranda and Shi Lin at the edge of the boat. "Where is he?" the mother asked.

"There." Shi Lin pointed to the inky, boiling water.

Miranda, blinking the tears out of her eyes, squinted into the darkness. There in the water was a patch of red—the backpack—and it was moving, heading steadily toward them.

"He's got his pack and slipped it on," Shi Lin said. "And now he's swimming back to us."

They watched as he moved several feet toward them—and then was driven away by a large swell. Once more, he began swimming in the direction of the boat—and once more, a wave took him away.

Miranda fell to her knees, closed her eyes, and wrung her hands together, but couldn't find the words with which to pray.

She rose back to her feet and shouted down to her brother. "Swim! Swim, Marko! You can do it. You can do it." Fearing her words were being carried away by the wind, she screamed them again as loud as she could.

"I'll get a rope and drop it down," said the woman, moving away.

* * *

The fight was over. Two hours had passed. An ash-covered, hyperexcited Yung Qui was carefully collecting details that he could add to his bottomless store of amazing tales to tell visitors.

He had just climbed on board the *Sparrow* to inform those on board that of the Pirate King's 25 ships, 7 had been captured, 10 burned, and the rest reduced to smoldering splinters, floating in the river.

Miranda sat in a dream, next to her soaked, dazed little brother, who was still clutching his torn backpack. She was stunned at what he had done. Nervous little Marko had leapt over a huge chasm between two ships, confronted the Pirate King, and then swum through shark-infested waters in the dark, all to recover the magic mirror.

How could he have done it? Was it magic? Or just courage? She knew that she herself wouldn't have had the nerve to do any of that—and yet, little, scared-of-everything Marko had grit his teeth and pulled off a miracle, an achievement that meant they still had a chance of returning to their lives, their world, their time.

Over the next hour, all the women and children on the *Sparrow* were transferred to the Treasure Ship.

The voyage out of the estuary, though short, was extremely difficult.

The storm had arrived with full force and the waters had become choppy. It had taken twenty minutes for the transfer boat to get close enough to the Treasure Ship to unload its final batch of human cargo.

Once on board, the ships' doctors looked at their wounds, all of which were thankfully minor. Those who needed to rest were sent downstairs, while the others were assigned to ready the ship to ride out the storm, battening down the hatches and roping down all loose objects.

The ships exited through the narrow inlet and were soon out in the open sea, heading for the nearest major harbor.

* * *

A deluge of rain fell all morning, and all hands were needed on deck, repairing the damage to the ship. The whole time, gusts of strong wind slammed the ship so hard that the shutters were torn from the windows and barrels of water tipped over.

As evening fell, Miranda, Marko, and Lin were summoned to the Admiral's office. He was sitting behind his desk, making a record of the battle. Although they were victorious, they had lost a lot of men, and Zheng He looked tired and unhappy. As they entered he glanced up and spoke in his gravelly voice, directing his comments at Miranda.

"Earlier, you said you were looking for someone?"

She nodded, but it was her brother who spoke. "Our grandfather," he said. "We need to find him. We're going to find him."

Miranda pulled out her locket. "This is what he looks like." She clicked it open and handed it to him. "Have you ever seen him?"

The large man's brow furrowed as he looked at the tiny image. "The painters in your land are highly skilled," he said, a tone of wonderment in his voice. "This looks so real I feel I could talk to this man."

Then he brought the small photograph closer to his face and his eyes widened in an expression of surprise and delight. "The Master. Your grandfather is the Master."

"You know him?" Miranda wanted to jump for joy. "Where is he? Do you know where he is? Is he on one of these ships?"

Zheng He shook his head. "I know him, yes, but I haven't seen him for many years—probably thirty or more. He could be anywhere in the world. Or he could be dead. He would be very old by now."

Miranda refused to let this disappointing answer upset her. "Please tell us everything you can about him. We're going to need every single clue we can get if we're going to have any chance of finding him."

The Lord of the Western Seas looked into the middle distance and scratched his bearded chin. "Where to begin?" he said. "You know ... your grandfather's story is intimately entwined with my own."

"Then tell us your story," said Marko.

The Admiral smiled. "Very well. I was born in Kunming, a city surrounded by mountains in an area known as the Land of Eternal Spring. I was a member of the people known as the Hui. You may wonder how a boy growing up in a landlocked place could dream of the sea. Well, it all started with my own grandfather ... and your grandfather."

He leaned back in his chair. "I'll always remember the stories my grandfather told me about how he and my father had sailed away on large vessels to faraway lands on sacred journeys, shortly after I was born."

"They went to a place called Mecca in the Arabian sands, on a journey called the Hajj. It was the joyful duty of all who believed in their faith, the faith of my fathers. Their stories and devotion inspired me to be a seeker, too. Later, I studied the wise sayings of Buddha, and then, I honored Tianfei, the Heavenly Goddess of the Sea. But the more I see the world, the more I realize that there is more on this planet than any of us can fathom … and more beyond this world, too."

"But our grandfather?"

"The face in the portrait belongs to the man who taught my grandfather and my father how to sail."

Marko and Miranda leaned forward, holding their breath.

The Admiral moved toward them and joined his hands together on the tabletop. "When I was about eight, a visitor from far away arrived at our home in the mountains. His clothes were strange, and so was his manner of speech. He was wise and mystical, like a prophet. People referred to him simply as the Master. He talked to the adults late into the night, and the next day my grandfather told me to spend as much time as possible learning from him. I remember staring at his face as he ate his noodles."

He leaned back and turned his head to stare out of the porthole. Although it was evening, the storm had turned the sky black. The sea was rough, and the room was visibly swaying. Zheng He's brush-pen rolled off the desk.

"I thought it strange that somebody said to be wiser than my grandfather could have a face without wrinkles. There was only a single deep crease that descended in a v-shape between his eyes. And I remember those eyes. They possessed a faraway look as if they were searching for something or someone miles away—or worlds away."

He picked the brush up from the floor.

"Your grandfather told me about the wonderful places he had seen on his travels. He told me about the amazing people he had met. He told me about the strange animals that lived around the world. He told me about a thousand marvels that made my jaw drop and my eyes bulge. He awoke in me a desire to travel, to see the world, to become wise. And he also told me about a God of Love, whose first followers were sailors, too—a bunch of simple fishermen. I had been a home-loving child before that, clinging to my mother's skirts when my father and his father went on their voyages. It was your grandfather who changed my attitude. From that day on, I begged my father to take me. The rest is history."

The door burst open. First Officer Ko stood in the doorway, his hair awry and his clothes soaked. "The storm is rising—you'd better come and see, sir."

The Admiral raised both palms in a gesture of reassurance. "Don't worry, children. We've survived a thousand storms."

But Ko shook his head. "With all due respect, this may be the one that breaks our good record, sir."

They raced upstairs.

The Light from Heaven

There was chaos on deck. The vessel was not only swinging from side to side, but was slowly tipping forward and backward. Its great size meant that its length spanned multiple waves, and it was being buffeted in all directions. Even the most experienced sailors were finding it difficult to remain upright without holding on to bolted-down objects.

The Admiral raced to the Chart Room, leaving Miranda and Marko in the care of Yung Qui.

A terrifying moaning sound could be heard: a roar of pain like a wounded dinosaur.

"What's making that howling noise?" Miranda asked. "Is it some sort of wild beast?"

"Yes, in a way. It's the timbers of the ship," Qui replied. "The sea is trying to tear it to pieces. The ship is in agony. It's screaming."

A huge roar prevented further speech. On the starboard side, a wave like a mountain flew to the sky, paused for a moment, and then crashed down like an avalanche, sending a small tidal wave across the deck.

"You must get below," he told them. "It's not safe here."

Miranda was not going to argue with that. She turned to head back the way they had come. But then she realized that her brother wasn't with them. She looked around but couldn't see him anywhere. "Marko? Marko? Where are you?"

Bursts of strong wind, unleashed by the gale, hit her face as if she was being pummeled by a prizefighter. She leaned into the stinging blasts, moving slowly toward the center of the deck, anxious to find her brother. "Marko! Marko!"

Then she saw him. He was standing calmly in the middle of the deck, looking upward at the storm. He looked utterly fearless, and there was something angelic, almost smiling, about his expression. He seemed to be contemplating, or perhaps praying.

She shouted at the top of her voice to be heard over the raging storm. "Marko, we've got to go down. It's not safe up here."

"I'll come in a minute."

Lightning cracked across the sky just above them, temporarily blinding her. When her sight recovered, she saw sailors racing to lower the sails.

There was movement behind her. Yung Qui fell to his knees. He was as terrified as she was, she realized. "This is no ordinary storm," he told her. "This storm is caused by the mother of all the sea dragons, the Great Goddess of the Sea herself. She is upset because of all the loss of life this past day. Go down and pray to your God."

"I can't leave without my brother," she said. The ship yawed dramatically to the port side, causing her to lose her balance completely. Just before she hit the deck, Qui reached out his long arm and yanked her over to a railing. Her knuckles turned white as she gripped as hard as she could.

A huge explosion filled the space above their heads and threw her to the ground. Raising her eyes, she realized that the lightning had hit the middle part of one of the masts. It was blackened and smoldering, the sparks shining in the dark. She heard a violent tearing sound, like a tree being ripped apart, and saw the mast was starting to disintegrate. The top half detached itself and started to descend.

Down, down, it fell, sending the sailors on the deck below scrambling for their lives.

Miranda watched in horror as it landed near Shi Lin, missing her by mere inches, and splintering the deck next to her. The young woman ducked her head to avoid the flapping batwing sails that came down with it, but stray ropes still attached to the mast slapped her like whips, wrapping themselves around her. She fell to the ground.

For a moment, the force of the ropes seemed to have slammed her into a state of unconsciousness. But then she revived and started struggling to free herself.

"Shi Lin's tangled in those ropes," Miranda shouted to Yung Qui.

The ship tilted to the starboard side and the broken mast began to roll, dragging Lin with it. She screamed and writhed, but was unable to free herself. "Help me!" she shrieked, as she was drawn toward the edge of the deck.

Another flash of lightning erupted overhead and Miranda saw a dark form rise from the shadows and race toward Lin.

It was Liang Dao Ming, the man in blue silk: the would-be King of Palembang. He raced to where she was lying on the deck and stood over her. Miranda could see that he was holding an ax. He lifted it high over his head.

"He's going to kill her," she squealed to Yung Qui. "Do something."

But they were too far away. There was no way they could reach them.

The ax came flying downward—and landed squarely on the ropes that bound Lin to the mast. Liang sliced down with his ax again and again and hacked the ropes to threads. Then he lifted Shi Lin free of her bonds, seconds before the remnants of the mast rolled away and fell over the edge of the ship, into the sea.

Lin stared at the man who had saved her life, but said nothing. He put her down, turned away and disappeared into the shadows. Lin carefully got to her feet and limped toward shelter. Yung Qui raced to help her.

Thunder boomed overhead but could not drown out the shouts of the sailors.

"Thank God," said Miranda as her brother suddenly appeared out of the darkness.

"Look," Marko said, pointing upward.

Admiral Zheng He had climbed onto the high podium—the place from which he had beaten the thunder drum to start the battle.

The great seaman seemed unperturbed by the strong hurricane winds swirling around the vessel. He lifted his hands to get the attention of the sailors.

"Fear not," he shouted. "Keep to your posts. This will pass."

Miranda suddenly smelled smoke. "The ship's on fire," she said.

"No," said Qui, who was carrying Shi Lin. "It's the sailors. They're burning offerings to the Goddess of Mercy."

Over the next few minutes, the wind gradually dropped and the roiling sea became calmer.

But as the storm started to die, something extraordinary started glowing in the air over the ship.

* * *

Miranda grabbed her brother's arm and pointed to the sky. "What on earth is that?" she wondered.

Yung Qui gasped. He put Shi Lin down and dropped to his knees again. "We must bow. It's the Goddess. It is Tianfei, come to show us her displeasure."

There was a large fireball in the air, close to the topmost mast. It glowed and sparked and fizzed with flames that were a lurid, greenish color. In the darkness of the cloud-covered evening, it throbbed with a painfully bright intensity.

As the wind dropped further, they could hear the sound it was making: the fireball hissed and sizzled and occasionally, made a sharp, cracking noise.

The thing, whatever it was, it was moving. It leapt from mast to mast. It seemed almost alive. And yet it was a real flame—even from a distance, Miranda could smell the ash as the wood of the masts was charred by the traveling blaze.

All around the ship, sailors fell to their knees and bowed their heads, murmuring prayers. Miranda dropped down to her knees, too, but out of fear, rather than worship. She noticed that Marko remained standing, his face turned up toward the light.

"Get down," Miranda shouted.

"Why should I?" Marko said. "The Admiral is still standing."

She looked up and realized he was right. Zheng He stood on his raised platform gazing at the light without fear. She raised herself up. "What is it?" she asked.

"I don't know," said her brother. "I think it may be St. Elmo's Fire."

"Meaning ... ?"

"St. Elmo's Fire ... it happens sometimes after a thunderstorm. Remember I was reading Ye Ye's book, *Strange Sea Phenomena*? It's got a whole chapter about this sort of thing."

The light was slowly lowering itself down the mast. The Admiral walked steadily toward it. It flashed brightly, and then disappeared. Darkness reclaimed the ship. The storm winds dropped to a light breeze. The sea became still.

On the high deck, Admiral Zheng He lit a lantern. His face looked ghostly as it reflected the light from the flame in his hand. His voice boomed out across the deck. "Today, near the end of our journey, we have beheld a great sign. Together, we have traveled more than a thousand miles through many watery worlds. We have seen waves rising before us like mountains touching the sky, and we have spied many marvels from countless secret lands hidden behind sea mists. Our sails spread out day and night like great clouds. They have carried us across these wild waves as swiftly as any shooting star, and as smoothly as a lone man's journey upon a clear highway."

The sea was now still. Hundreds of faces appeared from the shadows, and watched the Admiral as he spoke.

"We are travelers, all of us—fellow travelers along a single road. We have kept each other alive, both in body and in spirit. I tell you, the brightest stars are not to be found in the sky. They dwell aboard our humble rafts. For two long years you have shone, bright and brave, on journeys through unknown seas and undreamed-of lands, blazing a trail of discovery. The stars above us will burn forever. But so will the stars on this ship."

Wild cheering broke out, with hundreds of voices chanting the Admiral's name.

Shi Lin and Yung Qui did their best to cheer louder than anyone else.

Miranda was in a party mood. She kissed Shi Lin and then hugged Yung Qui, who blushed a deep shade of pink.

But then she became aware of someone tapping on her arm. She turned to find Marko next to her, his face very serious. "Look, Mira," he said. "See that light over there?"

The clouds had parted and a silvery white light was visible through the gap.

"It's moonshine ... a full moon."

An End and a Beginning

Miranda stared. He was right. A gap had opened in the storm clouds, and the moon was glowing in the sky.

After a storm, the sky always seems remarkably clear, and so it was on this occasion. She felt she could make out every single crater on the moon. But they were not standing in the moonlight. It was falling on the port bow side of the ship, some distance from where they stood.

"Quick," said Miranda. "Bring the bag."

There was no time to say any but the briefest of farewells to Shi Lin and Yung Qui, after which they raced down the creaking stairs and along the corridor. After three or four false leads, they managed to find a room with moonlight shining directly into it.

The circular porthole in the room reminded them of the round window in Ye Ye's office, and the miraculous way this adventure had started.

Marko pulled the magic mirror out of his bag and the two of them held it up to the porthole. The moon shone brightly through the bronze mirror, and the room became infused with a red-gold light.

Miranda noticed through her half-closed eyes that strange shapes were being projected on the walls of the cabin. She saw lines appearing on the ceiling. She saw a door projected onto the wall. She saw grid shapes coming into focus on the walls. She saw three-dimensional objects coming into focus in the room.

The light became intense.

"It's working," she whispered.

As she watched through half-shut eyes, the ghostly door she could see became sharp and solid. The grid shapes on the walls became Ye Ye's bookshelves. The transparent objects filled themselves in and became the desk and furniture of his room. Then the bright light faded and she opened her eyes fully. They were home, back in their grandfather's study.

"Home," said Marko.

"Home," echoed Miranda.

They picked themselves up and stared at the magic mirror.

"What was that all about?" said Marko. "Were we meant to travel to that place and find Ye Ye? Did we fail in our mission?"

Miranda shook her head. "I don't know. I just know that it was a pretty incredible adventure. I just wish ..."

"What?"

"I wish he'd left us a message or something so that we knew what was going on."

She walked over to the desk and started carefully examining the hinged box that the mirror had been in. Then she picked up the brown paper the parcel had been wrapped in and looked for clues. "I wish he'd included a letter or something."

"You said it yourself," said Marko. "Ye Ye always says, 'The action's at the edge.' He always likes to be really brave and go farther than anyone else. I guess he wants us to be like him."

"Easier said than done," his sister said. "He's a brilliant old man. We're just kids. We're not exactly cutting-edge people."

Marko blinked. "Hang on a minute. I've got an idea." He picked up the magic mirror and scanned its rim. "He's always going on about looking for the edge of things. Maybe he's written something on the edge of the mirror. There seem to be letters there."

The two children spent the next few minutes deciphering the words written around the edge of the bronze plate. Marko read the letters out while Miranda wrote them down. "It's a poem," she said, handing the piece of paper to her brother.

There are thirteen roads that could bring fear

And thirteen newborn moons this year

Take these paths and one will gain:

A hex, a jinx, a lifelong bane

"What does it mean?" Marko asked. "What do those words mean, 'hex,' and 'jinx,' and 'bane?' Are they types of treasure?"

"I don't know. I thought a jinx was a type of curse. But it can't be. Not if grandpa is behind this."

Miranda picked Ye Ye's calendar from his desk. "There are thirteen moons this year. And I think we've got thirteen lessons to learn. I think this is going to be a magical year."

Marko turned the mirror over and looked at its front surface again. "Interesting," he murmured. "There are lots of marked-off sections around the edge of the mirror. I'll bet there are wait, let me count them." His lips moved silently as he ran his fingers around the edge. "Thirteen?"

"Ten. Eleven. Twelve. Yep, thirteen."

"It figures," his sister said. "Maybe thirteen is a lucky number in ancient China."

"But these sections were all empty when we got it, I'm sure of it. Now one of them is filled. Look."

Miranda bent over the magic mirror to see a single Chinese calligraphy character carved into one of the thirteen sections. She read it out loud. "'Kan.' What does it mean?"

Marko shrugged. "*Kan* ... means ... 'Look.' Look at what? It could mean anything. Look out? Look inside a magic mirror? We need to find the rest of the characters before we can really know, I guess. Something tells me we have some big adventures ahead of us. We'd better be prepared."

He picked up his favorite history book from Ye Ye's shelf and chose one for his sister, too. "Homework," he said, heading out of the door.

Miranda followed, filled with excitement, innumerable thoughts running through her head every moment. "If Ye Ye is behind all this, then there's nothing to fear. He's just teaching us stuff in his weird and wonderful way."

Reaching the staircase, Marko turned to face his sister. "That was an amazing adventure," he said.

"You can say that again," she replied.

"But it's always nice to be home."

"I'd have to agree with that statement, too."

"Last one upstairs is a rotten egg."

"No fair! You're ahead of me."

The two children ran up the stairs.

* * *

In the study, the magic mirror glistened in its box.

A pair of eyes appeared in its surface and crinkled slightly, as if their owner was grinning. But they weren't the eyes of the children's grandfather. They were dark green eyes. And, had anyone been there to see it, they would have realized that it was unmistakably an evil grin.

In the deserted room, a voice mused to itself. "How nice. A new generation to carry the curse."

A Note from the Authors

Most of the events in this book actually happened. The story of Admiral Zheng He's life and the Treasure Ships; the battle with pirates and capture of the Pirate King Chen Zuyi; the storm and ghost light, are all based on real events that happened during the First Voyage of Admiral Zheng He, from 1405 to 1407. In 1409, the Admiral had a stone tablet engraved with these mysterious words that exist to this day:

In the third year of Yongle (1405) commanding the fleet we went to Calicut and other countries. At that time the pirate Chen Zuyi had gathered his followers in the country of Palembang, where he plundered the native merchants. When he also advanced to resist our fleet, supernatural soldiers secretly came to the rescue so that after one beating of the drum he was annihilated. In the fifth year (1407) we returned.

Who were these supernatural friends that came to help?

What kind of people followed Admiral Zheng He aboard the Star Raft, or raft of Treasure Ships? Many, like Yung Qui and the Admiral himself, may never have seen the ocean before, but they dreamed of departing on a journey to discover new and wonderful things.

As Nicholas D. Kristof writes in his *New York Times Magazine* article "1492: The Prequel," "In the end, an explorer makes history but does not necessarily change it, for this impact depends less on the trail he blazes than on the willingness of others to follow."

Follow the visionary voyage of Admiral Zheng He. Be an explorer yourself: Read more about voyages of discovery. And remember to look out for the next full moon and join Miranda and Marko when they meet a young traveler and listen to his strange tales of exploration and desert spirits in the second Magic Mirror adventure: *The Traveler's Tale*.

—*Luther Tsai and Nury Vittachi*

About the Authors

Luther Tsai has achievements worldwide as an architect, urban planner, author, and academic. From creating spaces in the most vibrant cities of modern Asia to creating innovative humanities, science, English, and Mandarin curriculums worldwide. Tsai and his wife, Serene Pang, the education consultant for this series, re-create the remarkable vision of ancient Asia found in the Magic Mirror series.

Nury Vittachi is an author based in Hong Kong. His writing is "endearingly wacky," said *The Times of London*, and "heading for cult status," according to the *Herald Sun* of Melbourne, Australia. Vittachi has had regular broadcasting slots on the BBC and CNN. *Doctor Who* star David Tennant recently recorded an audiobook version of a Vittachi tale.